Rainbow
ANIMAL HOSPITAL

Mango's Great Escape

Rainbow
ANIMAL HOSPITAL

Mango's Great Escape

Steve Attridge

Collins
An imprint of HarperCollinsPublishers

Rainbow
ANIMAL HOSPITAL

by Steve Attridge

For my son, Jacob.
Also, thanks to Ailsa McIntosh and all staff
at M.M. Leggett for their help.
Any factual errors remain mine alone.

First published in Great Britain by Collins in 1998
Collins is an imprint of HarperCollins*Publishers* Ltd
77-85 Fulham Palace Road, Hammersmith, London, W6 8JB

1 3 5 7 9 8 6 4 2

Text copyright © Steve Attridge 1998
Illustrations © John Bennett 1998

ISBN 0 00 6753590
The author asserts the moral right
to be identified as the author of the work.

Printed and bound in Great Britain by
Caledonian International Book Manufacturing Ltd,
Glasgow G64

Chapter One
A New Patient

It was September and Charlie the tortoise was preparing for her long winter hibernation.

Eddie Wright sometimes wished he could hibernate too, especially when there was a test at school, or he'd got into some sort of trouble and had to face his parents when he got home. If you hibernated for six months, the world would seem completely new and fresh when you woke up.

Eddie had first got to know Charlie when she'd needed X-rays to examine a growth. She was brought into Rainbow Animal Hospital by her elderly owners, Mr and Mrs Dobson. When Charlie had returned home, Eddie used to call on the Dobsons to see her. He also did a few odd jobs for the couple. That morning he'd been helping them build a pond in their garden. They had put in the plastic lining, plants and water, but now they needed to let it settle for a few weeks before they could put the fish in.

Before Eddie left the Dobsons to visit the hospital, he tickled Charlie under her chin. He loved looking at the perfect formation of rings on the segments of her shell. He tried to tempt her with a bit of tomato, but she wasn't hungry. She was just beginning to get drowsy. As her metabolism slowed down ready for her hibernation, so did her appetite. Eddie wondered if tortoises had a sense of time, the way people did. Or perhaps when Charlie woke up in the spring, it would just seem like it was the next day.

"Have a good kip, Charlie," he said and put her back in her wooden hutch. In a few weeks, when she was deeply asleep, she would be put in the garage and covered with straw. Eddie left her and cycled to the hospital.

*

Entering the hospital was like going home to Eddie. He loved it: the smells; the routines; the unexpected. He went through the double doors and smiled a 'hello' to his sister Chelsea, who worked in Reception. There were no patients and owners, so it was unusually quiet. Passing the familiar posters and photographs on the wall, Eddie went down the corridor to see Emma, the dog who lived at the hospital but whom everyone, even the grumpy chief vet, Mr Wensleydale, acknowledged as belonging to him. Emma came bounding across one of the wards as Eddie entered, licked him and wriggled like an eel with pleasure. Trundling behind her came Hannibal, an old bulldog, in a chariot which compensated for his crushed back legs. Eddie hugged him, smelling the rich doggy warmth of his fur, and the slightly less attractive, but no less loved, pong of his breath.

Then Eddie checked on some of the current patients: a squirrel with a broken leg, whose black eyes glittered through the cage at him; a cat with a cut paw; and a hedgehog who had got trapped in a lawnmower and almost starved because she couldn't get out. A few more decent meals of grubs and worms, another vitamin boost, and she would be set free. Eddie changed the bedding for the cat and fed Hannibal and Emma. Hannibal had to be restrained sometimes from helping Emma to finish her dinner too.

His chores done, Eddie went to say hello to Ron in the rest room. Ron, the ambulance driver, had his feet up and was sipping from a large mug that was so cracked and stained that no one else would use it. With his tea, he was nibbling a digestive biscuit. The biscuits were kept in a tupperware container and were meant to be for everyone. What happened, though, was that everyone else bought the biscuits, but only Ron ate them. He was extremely possessive about the biscuits and counted them every morning to make sure no one else had taken any. Eddie didn't bother to ask for one, because he knew the answer would be 'No'.

"Busy as usual, I see," Eddie said sarcastically.

"Been on duty since seven. No lunch break. This is the first time I've been able to have a cuppa and a nibble, so do me a favour and buzz off," said Ron.

Eddie was happy to 'buzz off' because he had heard voices in Reception, and voices probably meant a new animal. Eddie was gone before Ron could even grumble about what was wrong with young people today.

*

In Reception, a woman with wispy grey hair held a shoe box. Both she and Chelsea were peering into it.

"I tell you what, he's a lively little so-and-so," said the woman. "Look at that. Almost nibbled his way out. I reckon he was Houdini in another life, don't you?"

Eddie looked inside the box. An inquisitive, unafraid, small dark eye stared back at him. The other eye was closed. It was a pale-brown hamster, whiskers twitching, up on his back feet, front paws held in front of him, nose quivering – Eddie took in all the detail in a flash.

"Only got one eye but he don't miss a trick. Know where I found him?" asked the woman.

Eddie shook his head.

"In me crunchy nut cornflakes. Right

inside the packet, bold as brass and finished most of 'em an' all, I can tell you. Cheeky little so-and-so."

"So he's not yours?" asked Chelsea.

"No. Just turned up uninvited. Must have escaped from somewhere," said the woman, whose name was Martha Weston.

Eddie took the hamster from the box. He was careful to hold him with a hand cupped underneath, so as not to squash or frighten him. That way he would also avoid the possibility of getting nipped. The little creature stood up in Eddie's hand. He's used to being handled, Eddie thought.

Suddenly, the hamster ran up Eddie's arm, slid down his bomber jacket and landed in the pocket. Seconds later a hamster head popped out. He was holding a peanut which he had found there and started nibbling his prize.

This was one clever animal. Already Eddie could feel the familiar questions forming in his mind. What was his story? How did he come to be in Martha's house? To whom did he belong? If anyone was going to find out, it would be Eddie Wright.

Chapter Two

THE PROBLEM PATIENT

Eddie watched closely as Hilary David, one of the veterinary surgeons, examined the hamster.

"I wonder how he lost an eye," said Eddie.

"He hasn't. But he has got a bad case of conjunctivitis which has closed the left one. Look . . ." Hilary said, gently parting the hamster's left eyelids to reveal a rather sore-looking eye.

Life was full of surprises.

"So what are you going to do?" asked Eddie.

Hilary took a small tube from the medication cupboard and gently squeezed a little white ointment onto the hamster's left eye. He struggled and tried to wipe it off with his paws, then he licked them.

"Won't it give him bellyache, licking it like that?" asked Eddie.

"I think he'll be alright. Most animals are pretty clever at not eating things that are bad for them. Unlike people," she said, looking at Eddie's pocket which bulged with a packet of crisps, a tube of Rolos and a box of Nerds.

"Of course, we have got the same old

problem of what we are going to do with this little chap once he's well again, given that there appears to be no owner."

"Leave that to me and Kate," Eddie said.

Kate was Eddie's little sister, fierce as a piranha, clever as a dolphin, and good at finding things out.

Eddie took the hamster back to a small cage in the main ward. He decided to call him Hammy until he found out what his real name was. Eddie had already put some bedding in the cage and he spent the next ten minutes watching Hammy scurry about, busily building himself a nest. He had a strange habit of suddenly stopping and appearing to fall into a deep sleep for a minute or so, then snapping awake and busying himself again. He was very

quick and had soon turned the cage into a home. Now he clung to the bars and started nibbling them fiercely, possibly either to sharpen his teeth or to test the wire.

Eddie helped Greg to feed the other patients. Greg was a nursing assistant who was engaged to Eddie's sister, Chelsea. He was alright really, despite having a naff ponytail and a devotion to heavy metal music. Chelsea loved the ponytail, for some reason, but hated the heavy metal. She was already working on Greg to listen to Pavarotti. Eddie had no doubt she would get her way. For some reason when she fluttered her eyelashes or pouted her lips, Greg's brain seemed to turn to rice pudding and his only thought was to please her. It would be in such a mood that Pavarotti would emerge victorious on Greg's Walkman.

Eddie then took Emma for a run in the park. She was one of the fastest dogs he had seen, despite the fact that she'd once had a broken leg and a dislocated shoulder. Sometimes she ran so fast after a ball or a stick, then braked so hard when she'd caught up with it, that she tumbled over and over before running back. She was also proving to be a brilliant goalkeeper.

In the park was a marked football pitch. Eddie told Emma to sit on the goalie's line. She sat watching, a bundle of coiled energy ready to spring. Eddie walked to the penalty spot and put down the ball, all the time whispering 'Stay, stay. Good girl, stay'. Then he kicked the ball to her right or left and she dived. Nine times out of ten she would save the ball. She was so good Eddie nicknamed her 'Safe Paws'. Time flew.

When Eddie arrived back at the hospital he went to check on Hammy. To his horror, he found the cage was empty. As far as he could see, there was no way out, but when he opened the cage, there at the back, craftily concealed by the bedding, was a perfectly gnawed round hole. Eddie had noticed a tiny crack in the plastic at the back when he was preparing Hammy's new home, but didn't for a moment dream that he might bite through it. Astonishing! But also an emergency.

Eddie looked all round the ward, but couldn't find Hammy anywhere. He hoped he hadn't climbed into the cat's cage because he would probably have become a light snack. He looked under cages and cupboards, but Hammy had gone.

Chapter Three

THE HUNT IS ON

Eddie traced the possible routes Hammy could have taken. The nearest door was the one leading to the corridor. Off the corridor were Mr Wensleydale's room, Hilary's room, and the rest room. Mr Wensleydale, or Old Cheesy, as Eddie called him, always kept his door shut.

He was an old sourpuss, although even Eddie had to admit that Old Cheesy had been kind to him when his rabbit, Thumper, had died. Anyway, that door was closed. Hilary's door was closed too, as she had gone out on a call. That only left the rest room, unless Hammy had gone through to Reception.

"Seen the hamster anywhere?" Eddie asked Chelsea, in Reception.

"He hasn't escaped, has he?" she asked.

A woman, sitting in the corner with a budgerigar in a cage, looked down uncomfortably and lifted her feet from the floor. Eddie noticed this.

"'Fraid so, and you know what hamsters are like. Climb people's legs, get in their boxer shorts and all sorts," said Eddie.

The woman stood on her chair.

"I haven't seen him out here. Come

on, let's have a search," said Chelsea.

They looked in the treatment room behind Reception, but they couldn't find Hammy anywhere. Eddie was now starting to get worried. An animal as small as a hamster could easily get out without being noticed, or shut in a cupboard, or accidentally trodden on.

They went into the rest room. No one was there. All they could see were a few dirty mugs in the sink, a couple of newspapers on chairs, Greg's Sony Walkman and the tupperware biscuit box. Eddie and Chelsea looked under the chairs and table, and in the cupboard under the sink, but there was no Hammy. They were about to leave, when Eddie suddenly remembered Martha saying: "In me crunchy nut cornflakes. Right inside the packet, bold as brass, and finished most of 'em an' all,

I can tell you. Cheeky little so-and-so."
If Hammy could get inside a cardboard
box and chew his way out of a cage then
why not . . .

Eddie lifted the lid of Ron's
tupperware box. Sitting inside was
Hammy, holding a large chunk of
digestive biscuit and nibbling it happily.
His pouches were also full to bursting
point with biscuit. With his one good
eye he looked up at Eddie, startled,
twitched his nose and whiskers, then
carried on nibbling. In one corner was a
small chewed hole. There were quite a
few hamster droppings mixed with the
remaining biscuits.

"Little monkey," said Chelsea.

"Hamster, actually," corrected Eddie.
"If he can do all this with just one good
eye, imagine what he'll be like with
two!"

"Ron is not going to be pleased when you tell him," said Chelsea.

"You're the one with the toothpaste smile that blokes go all daft over. You tell him," said Eddie.

They tossed a coin and Eddie lost. He would have to tell Ron. Eddie took Hammy back to the ward. He looked in the storeroom and found a more durable metal cage and put Hammy's bedding in it, then Hammy himself. Finally, he gave Hammy another dose of eye ointment, which the little hamster did not like at all. It was five o'clock. He'd go home for tea, have a planning talk with Kate, then they would try to find out where Hammy came from.

Then Greg came in. When Eddie told him about Hammy's great escape, he laughed.

"Maybe we should put a ball and

chain on him," said Greg.

"Right. Do you think Chelsea will make you wear a ball and chain when you get married?"

Greg's face went red. Eddie loved winding him up.

"What do you mean?" he asked.

"I just mean that she's a dead jealous sort of person. Gets this red mist and becomes sort of uncontrollable. Obviously she hasn't done it with you yet," said Eddie.

"No. What do you mean – uncontrollable?" asked Greg, half knowing he was being wound up, but not completely sure.

"Oh, you know, she just sort of lashes out in a mad rage. Hit one bloke in a pub once."

"Eddie, you must think I'm stupid to believe that," said Greg with a snort, but Eddie noticed that Greg's eyes were a little nervous.

Then the telephone rang in Reception and moments later Chelsea came in with a message for Eddie. It was a day for losing things. Eddie wasn't going to get home for another two hours, at least.

Chapter Four

ANOTHER HUNT

Mr and Mrs Dobson were in a terrible state. Charlie had disappeared.

"There's nowhere she could have got out of the garden, nowhere at all," said Mr Dobson over and over again.

Mrs Dobson couldn't keep still. She kept going in and out of the garden in the hope that the tortoise would suddenly appear. She had gone to check that Charlie was OK that morning, but she wasn't there. They had hunted round the garden dozens of times before telephoning the Rainbow Animal Hospital. Eddie listened, then went out into the garden.

Charlie's hutch was certainly empty. Eddie looked round the garden. There were a few large shrubs – given that tortoises were burrowing creatures it might be worth digging down a bit to investigate. There were no holes in the fence as far as Eddie could see.

It wasn't impossible that someone had stolen Charlie. When Charlie was in the hospital having her X-rays, Hilary told Eddie that there was an import ban on tortoises. An old-timer like Charlie was worth a lot of money, and would maybe fetch three or four hundred pounds. So any tortoise being offered for sale would be worth investigating.

Eddie moved into action quickly. He rounded up his sister Kate, his best mate Imran and a couple of other friends, Matt Miller and Mike Hardingale. Kate and Imran knocked on every door in the road to ask if anyone had seen Charlie and whether they could have a quick look in their garden. If anyone objected, Kate gave them such a steely, contemptuous look that they instantly relented, inviting her and Imran in and offering drinks and biscuits – anything to stop this fierce little girl from looking at them like that.

Matt and Mike did a tour of the local pet shops, asking if anyone had been offering a tortoise for sale.

Eddie made a few phone calls, including one to the local radio station. Within minutes a DJ announced: "Anyone out there seen Charlie the tortoise? If so, either contact Radio Central or phone Rainbow Animal Hospital."

An hour later they had got no further. The children sat in the kitchen with Mr and Mrs Dobson and tried to think what to do next. They decided to widen the search the next day, and to put notices around the area. For now they had done all they could. They made some notices:

TORTOISE
CALLED
CHARLIE (FEMALE)
MISSING

Anyone with any information please contact
Mr and Mrs Dobson, 14 Lea Way Tel 367291
Charlie is about to hibernate, so if you find her
please treat her carefully.

On their way home, the children taped the notices on lampposts. Eddie and Kate decided they just had time to call in on Martha to make a few enquiries about Hammy.

Martha recognised Eddie and let him and Kate come in.

"How is he then?" she asked.

"Fine. He *has* got two eyes, but one was closed because he had conjunctivitis. It's a lot better now. We were just wondering how he might have got into your house," said Eddie.

"We're a bit hungry too," said Kate. "We haven't had our dinner 'cos we've been busy looking for a tortoise."

"Have you now?" said Martha, eyeing Kate.

Martha fetched a packet of biscuits. She put about a dozen on a plate and offered them to Eddie and Kate. Eddie took two and Kate took six. Rather than being annoyed, Martha seemed to find it all quite interesting. Kate ate the biscuits, then took the remaining four.

"You're a bit like that hamster yourself, aren't you?" said Martha to Kate. "Bloomin' hungry. Got worms, have you?"

"Snakes," said Kate, finishing the last biscuit. "Right, let's have a look where you found him."

Martha showed them her walk-in pantry. There were shelves packed with tins, packets and bottles. A large fridge stood just inside the door. Eddie and Kate looked round. Kate noticed a packet of jam tarts and showed an unusual amount of interest in them. Eddie looked in the corners to see if there were any holes where Hammy might have entered. He peered behind the fridge and there on the skirting board was an old mouse hole. Or possibly a hamster hole.

"What's on the other side of the wall here?" asked Eddie.

"Next door. It'd lead to Frank and Ivy Ferris's. They never owned a hamster, not that I knew of," said Martha.

Eddie and Kate thanked Martha, then went and knocked next door. There was no one at home, so they decided to try again the next day. It had been a tiring day and although Eddie didn't yet know it, tomorrow was going to be far more difficult than he could imagine.

Chapter Five

RON'S BIG MISTAKE

Mr Wensleydale was in a bad mood. He had to go to a meeting, he was late, and it seemed to be everyone's fault except his own. He came out of his room looking harassed, a briefcase in one hand, a small suitcase in the other.

"*Now* I can't find my glasses," he said

irritably.

"You're wearing them, Mr Wensleydale," said Greg.

Eddie sniggered. Usually Old Cheesy was so organised, but as he walked away, Eddie glanced in his room and noticed the IN tray was crammed with paperwork.

"By the way, I want a word with you," said Greg, as he and Eddie walked away.

Eddie knew from the tone that Greg didn't want *a* word at all, he wanted hundreds, perhaps thousands, of them.

"I asked Chelsea about hitting some bloke in a pub and she said she'd never hit anyone in her life. In fact she was quite annoyed," Greg said.

"Yeah, she's always been worried that you might find out about her little . . . problem," said Eddie.

"What problem?" asked Greg, despite himself.

"Oh, nothing. Just . . . she has these sort of moods where she . . . I really shouldn't say."

"You can say, because I don't believe you," said Greg.

"No point in me telling you then. But don't blame me when she goes berserk and cuts off your ponytail," said Eddie.

"She doesn't like my ponytail?" asked Greg. "She's never said anything to me."

"Probably doesn't want to hurt your feelings," said Eddie.

"But she really has said to you that she doesn't like it?" asked Greg, completely hooked by now.

"Says you look like the back end of a shire horse," said Eddie. "Quite witty really, for Chelsea."

Eddie left Greg to his own thoughts

and went to do his daily chores: feed and walk Emma; feed and cuddle Hannibal; make sure bedding supplies were in order; mop the ward floor. He also checked on Hammy, who was curled up and sleeping so deeply that at first Eddie thought he might be dead. Hammy opened one sleepy eye when Eddie tapped the bars of his cage, then he fell asleep again, curled into a tight little ball.

Then Eddie went to the rest room. Now that the tupperware biscuit box was ruined and Hammy had left his droppings in it, he had been meaning to throw it away. He had also forgotten to tell Ron what had happened. But when he entered the rest room Ron was sitting with the box on his lap, just finishing off the last of the biscuit bits. Eddie gaped at him.

"Someone's been at the biscuits," said Ron, putting the last handful of crumbs and droppings in his mouth. "Was it you?"

Eddie shook his head.

"Well, someone did, 'cos they was all broken and there was these dried currants in here too," said Ron, chewing vigorously.

"Currants?" asked Eddie feebly.

"Yes. Bit chewy, but I've tasted worse."

Now some people might have told Ron that he'd just eaten hamster droppings. Some people might say that Ron should be told. Some people might even say that it would be cruel not to tell Ron. But Eddie wasn't some people. He decided that if anyone was going to tell Ron, it certainly wasn't going to be him, though it might be fun to tell a few other people. And as a gesture of friendship, Eddie would keep an eye on Ron to see if he suffered any serious after effects.

Within ten minutes Chelsea, Greg, and another nurse, Kalim, knew, and for the rest of the day Ron had the feeling that people were laughing at him whenever his back was turned.

On his way home, Eddie called in at Mr and Mrs Dobson's house. He, Kate, Imran, Matt and Mike all arrived and planned the next part of their campaign to find Charlie. There had been no response to the radio announcement, nor to the posters. The consensus now was that Charlie had been taken or, more likely, had burrowed somewhere. They decided to dig around all the bushes and shrubs in the garden.

They had just started digging when Eddie heard a small 'Oh no!', like a gasp, from Mrs Dobson. She was standing by the pond, looking down in a horrified trance. Eddie walked over to her, half knowing what he would see.

He was right. There at the bottom of the pond was Charlie the tortoise.

Chapter Six
A TRAGEDY

They all gathered round and watched solemnly as Eddie lay flat on the ground and reached into the water. Charlie's body was heavy, so he needed both hands to gently lift her from the pond. Even Kate, who nearly always had something to say, was silent. Mr

Dobson held his wife's arm. Charlie's head was withdrawn into her shell, but her four legs drooped lifelessly, water streaming from them. It must have been an agonising and horrible death, Eddie thought, as he lay her on the grass and brushed water from her shell.

"It's horrible. Poor thing!" said Mrs Dobson, as she burst into tears.

"She was always a curious one. Must have lost her balance," said Mr Dobson.

Mrs Dobson wiped her eyes with a small, embroidered hanky. Eddie noticed that her hand trembled.

"And to think that all the time we were looking for her, she was there. If we'd found her straight away we might have saved her," she said.

"I'm really, really sorry," said Eddie.

"Thanks for all your help anyway. You couldn't have done more," said Mr Dobson.

They all looked at the still and silent body, glistening with pond water.

"We can still help," said Kate. "Charlie needs a proper funeral. We'll help you."

And that is exactly what they did. It was better to be doing something – there was something unbearable about just standing and looking at poor Charlie. Kate and the boys dug a hole. Imran collected some stones. Then they put Charlie in the hole and made a burial mound above her. Imran arranged the stones on top of the mound into the shape of a C, for Charlie. They they stood quietly for a minute or so. No one really wanted to say anything, so they were just silent.

It was time to go. Eddie promised to call in the next day just to say 'hello'.

He knew what it was like having a pet die. His very own pet at the hospital, Thumper the rabbit, had died not long ago. Eddie remembered the silkiness of his ears, his wonderful coat, the twitch of his whiskers and his sense of fun. In a secret part of himself, Eddie still missed Thumper grievously. Perhaps he always would. Maybe you never really get over someone close to you dying – perhaps they lived on inside you in some way it was difficult to think about, but possible to feel. So Eddie felt for Mr and Mrs Dobson. They might want to talk about Charlie, so he would make sure he called in as often as he could.

Eddie arranged to meet Kate later at Martha's neighbour's house to continue their quest for Hammy's owner. Then he cycled back to the hospital to give Emma a short walk. On the way there, he thought how strange it was that nobody can teach you about how it feels to die. There was tons of information on how to look after animals, and at school everything was about living things, but nobody ever said much about dying. Presumably because nobody knew, or because it was too scary to think about. Everybody wanted to live forever, Eddie supposed, even grumpy people who behaved as if having fun was a crime.

At the hospital, Chelsea was just going off duty. She walked past Eddie without saying a word. Strange, he thought. Usually Chelsea wouldn't shut up. Eddie had even bought Greg a pair of ear plugs as an engagement present, which, for some reason, hadn't been too popular with anyone. Then Greg walked past and Eddie had to do a double take.

The familiar swing of the ponytail was gone and there was a newly cropped Greg.

"Is that you?" asked Eddie. "What have you done? You look like a coconut."

"And you'll look like a pancake once I flatten you," said Greg bitterly.

"Why me? What have I done?" asked Eddie.

"Done. What have you done? This is what you've done!" snapped Greg pointing to his cropped hair. "You said Chelsea hated my ponytail so I had it all chopped off and now she'll barely speak to me. She said she loved my long hair. She thought *I* knew that and had it cut off just to show her I could do what I liked. I was actually trying to please her! And it's all your fault, Eddie Wright."

If Eddie could have a pound for every

time he'd heard that last phrase he'd be as rich as a lottery jackpot winner.

"Why was it my fault? You've got a mind of your own, haven't you?" said Eddie. "If I'd said Chelsea wanted you to stick your head in the oven, you wouldn't have done that, would you?"

Greg went off in a bad mood and Eddie was left to think again how stupid adults were when they were in 'lurve'.

Hilary David came out of her room and started to chat to Eddie. He told her about Charlie and how horrible it had been. As they chatted they passed Mr Wensleydale's room. The door was open, which was odd, but Eddie remembered that Old Cheesy had been in such a bad-tempered hurry that he'd rushed off and left it open. As he closed the door, he noticed that the IN tray which had been stacked high with papers, was now nearly empty and that the floor was a litter of scraps of paper.

"I think there's a problem," he said.

They entered and there *was* a problem. Most of the papers were ruined.

"But who did it?" asked Hilary. "Have we got mice?"

"No," said Eddie, "but we have got a hamster."

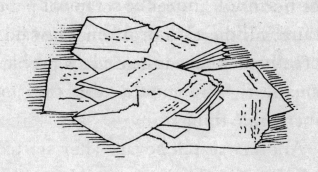

Chapter Seven

ANOTHER SEARCH

Hammy's cage was empty, as Eddie knew it would be. The door was off its hinges. One of them must have been weak and Hammy had chewed and chewed until the door opened. It was amazing how determined and resourceful such a little animal could be, although a couple of years of being at the hospital – during most waking non-school, non-chore hours – had taught Eddie that often it was the creatures that appeared weakest or smallest who could do the most incredible things.

Another search began. They started in Mr Wensleydale's room. Hammy had obviously got on the desk somehow. Presumably once he'd had a happy time shredding all the paperwork and dropping some of it on the floor, he'd got down again. Eddie looked under the desk, under the bookcase, but no Hammy.

Kalim was called in and she began looking in other parts of the hospital. Hilary tried to salvage some of the paperwork. She held up a ragged, tooth-marked piece of a cheque.

"Our little patient has destroyed invoices, letters, order forms and about four hundred pounds worth of cheques," she said.

"Yeah. Hammy doesn't do things by halves. When he starts something he really does a good job," said Eddie.

"Mr Wensleydale is going to go ballistic about this," said Hilary.

"Then Mr Wensleydale should provide better housing for the patients," said Eddie. "Housing they can't escape from."

"And what else should Mr Wensleydale do, so that the hospital is run according to the likes and beliefs of the illustrious Eddie Wright?" said Mr Wensleydale as he entered the room and heard Eddie's last remark.

Eddie blushed. Why did things like this always happen to him, he wondered, deciding it was best to say nothing for the moment.

"I thought you had a meeting," said Hilary.

"Cancelled, like that cheque you're holding, to judge by the state of it. Sabre-toothed squirrel, was it? Alligator? Grizzly bear?"

"A hamster," said Hilary. "Remember – conjunctivitis? Came in a few days ago? No traceable owner."

"To which we can now add: a propensity for wanton violence, hooliganism and unprovoked attacks on my IN tray," said Mr Wensleydale, who often preferred to use a dozen words where one would do.

After another look round the office, Hilary and Eddie were shooed out. As the door closed they could hear a chair being kicked furiously inside. Old

Cheesy always gave something a good boot when he was angry, which is why filing cabinets, chairs, cupboards and desks all over the hospital had little dents in them. Eddie found it odd that Old Cheesy could be like that, yet when he was with the animals he always showed patience and concern, and could perform the most delicate operations.

Eddie had once seen him set the broken leg of a frog and he'd marvelled at the surgeon's skill and dexterity. Definitely a funny mixture, Old Cheesy.

Kalim hadn't found Hammy. The hamster was still missing at five o'clock, which was when Eddie had promised to meet Kate. He hated leaving the hospital without finding him, but Kalim said she would telephone a message through to

Eddie's house if he was found. Wherever Hammy was, once the hospital was locked for the night, he would hopefully be safe until morning, when they could have another look.

Eddie cycled as quickly as he could to meet Kate. She was sitting on a wall outside Martha's neighbour's house. He told her about Hammy's latest disappearance, then they knocked at the door. A woman with a long nose and small black eyes opened it. She looked from Kate to Eddie.

"Mrs Ferris? Mrs Ivy Ferris?" asked Kate, who had a way of making people feel guilty even when they hadn't done anything.

"Yes," she said.

"We're on a mission. We're trying to trace the owner of a hamster who was found by your neighbour," said Kate.

"We looked in her kitchen and we're pretty sure that he got into her house from yours, so we were wondering if you knew anything," asked Eddie.

"Not me. Frank!" she called.

Moments later another face appeared, a man's, and he too had a long nose and small black eyes. Like a pair of rats, thought Eddie, who liked rats and thought them much maligned animals, so it was a sort of compliment.

"Know anything about a hamster?" asked Ivy.

"No. Should I?" he said.

"Do you mind if we come in to see if Hammy did actually come from your house?" asked Kate, then added, "And have you got any biscuits or crisps, because we haven't eaten anything today. Our mum and dad are too poor to feed us until the evening."

Eddie looked at Kate. Even though she was his sister and he knew her so well, Kate's lies, told with such conviction and innocence, always took him by surprise.

Mrs Ferris wasn't convinced that this was a good idea. Neither was Mr Ferris.

"I don't think so," he said. "Children get in the way. They break things and don't pay for them."

It did not look as if Eddie and Kate were going be allowed in, then Eddie looked past Mr Ferris and into the kitchen.

"Walking sticks," he said.

Mr Ferris looked at him.

"You like them?" he asked.

"Of course," said Eddie.

"Then come in and have a look. I've got some pretty interesting characters in here," said Mr Ferris.

Eddie entered. Kate followed, wondering what on earth all this stuff about walking sticks was.

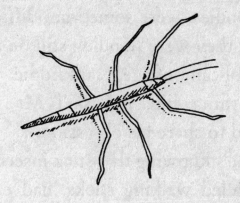

Chapter Eight

FOLLOWING THE TRAIL

The Ferris kitchen was like a glass house. On every available surface, including the table, chairs, shelves and cupboard tops, were aquariums. Inside the aquariums were leaves, grasses and twigs, and dozens and dozens of stick insects. Kate and Eddie peered inside at the creatures who, with their strange twig-like legs and long bodies, were sometimes difficult to spot if they were standing still on a twig.

"Cool camouflage," said Eddie.

"Nothing like it," said Mr Ferris, pleased to share his obsession.

Eddie's knowing that stick insects were also called walking sticks, had ensured his and Kate's entry into the Ferris household.

"Over here, I've got some leaf insects too. See?" Mr Ferris said, indicating to what looked to Kate like an aquarium of leaves. Then one of the leaves moved.

"Enlargements of the leg and abdomen that make them resemble leaves. Cunning, eh?"

"You and your bloomin' stick insects. One of these days you'll turn into one yourself," said Mrs Ferris.

Eddie noticed that she said it in a way

which meant she didn't really mind at all.

"Everyone likes fluffy little things for pets, all big eyes and fur, but these creatures are alright too. *I* like 'em anyway," said Mr Ferris.

"Er, speaking of fluffy little things, could we have a look at where Hammy might have got into Martha's house?" asked Kate.

"Help yourself," said Mr Ferris.

"And about those biscuits?" added Kate.

Mrs Ferris opened a packet of bourbons and Kate took four.

Eddie knelt down and looked at the wall on the other side of which was Martha's house. And there, behind the cooker, was a small mouse or Hammy-shaped hole. "That's it!" said Eddie.

"Well, blow me," said Mr Ferris, kneeling down and looking. "But if he went through there, how did he get into

our house in the first place?"

"He's pretty small and pretty clever too," said Eddie. "He could have come under the floorboards, maybe even along the roof. Who knows?"

Mrs Ferris had a thoughtful look on her face.

"I remember now – several mornings I kept finding bits chewed off the newspaper. Thought it might be mice, but . . ."

"But it was probably Hammy, and—" Eddie stopped as he had a sudden realization. He turned to Kate. "I know where Hammy is. I'm so stupid. Why didn't I think of it before?"

Eddie turned to Mr and Mrs Ferris.

"Thanks! Great help, but we've got to go."

Kate shrugged her shoulders and followed him out. Just after they'd left

the house, Kate noticed a girl of about her own age entering next door.

"Come on!" shouted Eddie, cycling away.

"I'll see you later. Got a hunch about something," said Kate.

Kate's hunches were usually worth following. Sometimes they led to difficulties – even danger, but they were always interesting.

With a last wave at Mr and Mrs Ferris Eddie cycled back to the hospital as fast as he could. Going downhill he went so fast he overtook a man on a moped. It was tempting to reach out and take the man's cap from his head, but although the thought passed through Eddie's mind, he decided he had more important business to attend to. This was no time to get into unnecessary trouble.

Chapter Nine

ALMOST IN TIME

It was so obvious. Eddie wondered why his brain had been asleep when he had been in Old Cheesy's office. The piles of paper chewed up wasn't an act of 'hooliganism' at all, it was a small creature thinking carefully about making a bed. That's why Hammy had chewed

up the papers. And he would have chosen a place nearby, so that he didn't have to carry the paper in his pouches too far. Eddie was pretty sure he knew where Hammy had decided to make his bed.

Eddie left his bike outside the hospital on its side, the back wheel still spinning madly as he pushed open the double doors of the hospital. Chelsea gave him a stern look as he passed through Reception – presumably Greg had blamed the disastrous haircut on Eddie. Why did everyone always blame him? He gave her the sweetest smile he could muster and went down the corridor. He knocked on Old Cheesy's door and entered without waiting for a reply.

Cheesy was at his desk trying to sellotape some of the ruined letters together again. He wasn't making a

good job of it, considering he was a surgeon.

"What the . . .?!" said Old Cheesy.

"Sorry, it's just that I think I know . . ." said Eddie as he went to the desk and, yes, one of the drawers was slightly open. Just enough for a hamster to get in and build a nest. Eddie opened the drawer and there was a great fluffy ball of paper, a perfectly built nest, made up from scraps of receipts, cheques and letters.

"How did you know he'd gone there?" asked Mr Wensleydale, peering inside the drawer.

"Elementary, dear sir, I'm a natural genius," said Eddie, thinking that his brilliant powers of deduction had earned him the right to be a bit cheeky, even to Old Cheesy.

"Hamsters are home builders, aren't

they? Even wandering Hammies like our one. But the trouble is – he's not at home. Blow!" said Eddie, looking through the nest. It almost felt as if Hammy had known his new nest would be discovered and he'd gone walkabout. They would have to start searching all over again.

While Eddie had gone back to the hospital, Kate had gone to the next house along from Mr and Mrs Ferris, where she had seen the girl. She knocked at the door and the girl answered.

"Hi," said Kate.

The girl looked at her.

"My name's Kate and I'm probably the most intelligent person you've talked to all day, so make the most of it."

This got the girl's interest. Kate asked for her name.

"Aruna," she said. "What do you want?"

"Rather, it's what *you* want," said Kate, enjoying the situation. She loved keeping people guessing.

"What do I want?" asked Aruna.

"My help," said Kate.

"What for?"

"Because without it you might never see him again," said Kate.

"See who?" asked Aruna.

"Him who you lost."

"Who's that?"

"A hamster."

The girl's eyes widened.

"You found Mango?!" she asked, desperately wanting to believe Kate, but worried in case it wasn't true.

Kate congratulated herself on being

right – Hammy did belong to the girl. She explained what had happened and it was all she could do to stop Aruna going straight down to the hospital there and then. This would have been a problem, because Kate hadn't yet told her that Hammy, or rather Mango, was lost. She didn't want to upset her even more than she obviously had been. But Kate had complete faith in herself and Eddie finding Mango before tomorrow. Aruna said she would come to the hospital after school to collect Mango.

"But why didn't you tell her? S'pose we don't find . . . Mango," said Eddie, half an hour later, as he and Kate left the hospital, wheeling their bikes.

He had looked everywhere for Mango, with no luck. He still thought of him as Hammy, but Mango was a pretty

cool name, wherever he was.

"Don't be such a pestilence," said Kate.

"You mean pessimist," said Eddie. "I'm just saying that if we don't find him and this Aruna turns up it's going to be ten times worse for her. She'll be losing him all over again."

"Then that settles it. We definitely have to find him. You finish school early on Fridays so get straight down to the hospital and have a good shifty."

And with that, Kate got on her bike and rode away.

"Thanks," said Eddie to himself. Of course, he had no idea that very soon something was going to happen that even he would find difficult to believe. One of the strangest things ever. And it had nothing to do with Mango.

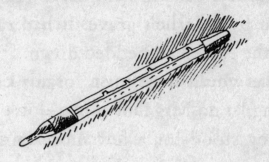

Chapter Ten

SURELY THIS ISN'T HAPPENING

Mr and Mrs Dobson were glad to see Eddie. Mr Dobson half thought that they wouldn't see him again, now that Charlie was gone, but Eddie was there now in their kitchen eating a Kit-Kat and telling them about Mango. After a while he suggested that they go out into

the garden. The three of them went and stood by Charlie's grave. It had rained and the earth had bedded down.

"She would have been forty-six next spring," said Mrs Dobson.

They stood for a few more minutes. Eddie noticed that the pond in which poor old Charlie had drowned had been taken away. He guessed there wouldn't be another one, not while the Dobsons were there.

They turned away to go back indoors when something caught Eddie's eye. A slight tremor. A movement in the earth. He turned back and could swear that Charlie's grave moved slightly. He must have been mistaken. But then it moved again. A mole? Insects? Then with a shove the unmistakable claw of a tortoise pushed through the earth.

Eddie's jaw opened but he couldn't

make a sound. This was bizarre, like something out of a horror book; *Tortoise from Beyond the Grave* or *The Claw from Hell*. The claw lay there for a moment, then scraped and pushed, as if to get a grip. The earth broke and another claw appeared. Eddie closed his eyes tight, then opened them again. This really was happening.

"Coming in, Eddie?" asked Mr Dobson.

Eddie could only point feebly. Mr Dobson looked and pointed too, his eyes as wide as Eddie's. Mrs Dobson looked and started to faint, but Mr Dobson caught her. Eddie raced over and started to scrape away the earth. Mr and Mrs Dobson joined him, the three of them on their knees with their fingers in the soil. And there, moments later, like a struggling, spluttering, newly-

born thing, was Charlie. Mrs Dobson lifted her triumphantly, muttering 'Charlie, Charlie, Charlie. You're back! You're back!'

Charlie was caked in dirt. It was in her eyes, in all her joints, in her mouth. She spat earth and tried to scrape it from her pink tongue with her claws.

"Take her in the kitchen, Joyce," said Mr Dobson.

They took Charlie to the kitchen and wrapped her in a clean tea-towel to get the worst of the dirt off, and because she was very cold. Mrs Dobson got a damp cloth and began wiping the earth from her face and claws. Mr Dobson ran some lukewarm water in a washing-up bowl. Eddie gently put her in the water and they gave her a bath to ease her joints. She looked blearily around, her eyes filmy. She spat feebly as if

thoroughly disgruntled by her ordeal.

"I can't believe it," said Mr Dobson.

"We buried her. She was a goner," said Eddie.

"And she was in that pond for nearly twenty-four hours before that. I can't see how anything could survive that long underwater unless it was a fish," said Mr Dobson.

"And then we buried her, so she had another twenty-four hours without air," said Mrs Dobson. The enormity of what she had just said hit her and she had to sit down. Tears sprang to her eyes.

"Charlie, what did we do? We buried you alive," she said, still wondering if this was a dream.

"But she seemed dead. She looked dead. She was dead! Wasn't she?" asked Mr Dobson.

Charlie had obviously decided that

she most definitely was not dead, and was fed up with all these questions. Her eyes were slightly unfocussed, and she seemed to have used up all her strength surviving her ordeal and struggling free. Now she was exhausted. Eddie thought she might still be in danger. She was about to hibernate when she went through the most amazing death-defying experience, so much of her energy and resources that she needed to survive a long winter must have been used up.

"I think we should get her to the hospital for a checkup," said Eddie.

Chapter Eleven

A TRICKY TIME WITH GREG

"It's an extraordinary story," said Hilary as she checked Charlie's heart rate and body temperature.

Charlie was very still, and Eddie thought that if she had any energy she would tell them all to shut up so she could get on with the serious business

of sleeping for six months.

"She is weak. Her muscles are tired and I imagine her central nervous system has taken quite a shock," said Hilary.

"But she made it, didn't she?" said Mr Dobson with a hint of pride, and tapping her shell gently.

"She certainly did," said Hilary.

"What are you going to do for her?" asked Eddie.

"I think a vitamin boost to get her strength up and replace what she lost, then let her rest somewhere warm. Gradually she'll return to her own hibernation pattern."

"I still don't understand how she survived," said Mrs Dobson. "She was in the water a day and a night, before she was buried. How could she breathe? And it was freezing."

Hilary thought for a moment. "I think that once she was in the pond and realised she couldn't get out, she went into a deep hibernation state, her heart barely beating, so that she could just tick over. That's why you thought she was dead. But it's still pretty amazing. There aren't many weeks that go by in this job when I'm not surprised by something or other."

The crisis was over. Charlie was going to be all right. Now that Eddie knew, he went off to feed Emma and take her for a walk. He also gave Hannibal a slobbery cuddle and stopped him eating everyone else's dinner, then he went to see how the search for Mango was going.

He found Greg in one of the wards, bottle-feeding a kitten whose mother had been killed in a road accident.

"Cool haircut," said Eddie, unable to resist the jibe.

"Eds, you don't know when to stop, do you? It's going to take months for it to grow again."

"Wear a wig," said Eddie.

Greg's expression told Eddie it was time to stop the mickey-taking.

"So, are things all right with Chelsea again?" asked Eddie.

"Yes. No thanks to you," said Greg.

Time to change the subject, thought Eddie.

"I don't s'pose anyone's found Mango?" he asked.

"Not a whisker," said Greg. "He didn't return to that nest in Mr Wensleydale's office, and no one's seen him anywhere in the hospital."

"Tricky. His real owner's coming to collect him tomorrow. Girl called Aruna,"

said Eddie.

"But she knows he's gone AWOL, doesn't she?"

"Er, not exactly," said Eddie.

"What do you mean – not exactly?" asked Greg.

"I mean . . . no," said Eddie.

"Then you'd better tell her," said Greg.

"That won't be necessary."

"Why not?"

"Because I'm going to find Mango."

"How?"

"Somehow," said Eddie, who had no idea how he was going to find the little hamster. No idea at all.

That evening he spoke to Kate and they agreed that although Eddie would continue the search as planned, Kate would go to fetch Aruna and break the sad news that Mango was missing.

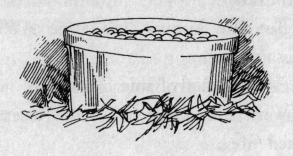

Chapter Twelve

THE BIG MOMENT APPROACHES

Eddie had tried everything, but now he'd run out of ideas. It was Friday at four o'clock. He had been at the hospital since two. After taking care of Emma and helping with the other animals he had another look for Mango in the wards, in Reception, the rest room, all with no

luck. He'd looked in cupboards, the stock room and the laundry baskets. He was now coming to the conclusion that Mango had probably gone for good. Maybe he'd scuttled across Reception when no one was looking and got out when the front door was open. Perhaps, and Eddie didn't like to consider this but he realised he might have to, perhaps one of the patients had caught and eaten Mango.

Eddie had put down food in the hope that it would attract Mango, but the food lay untouched, so now he let Hannibal hoover it up with his great wet jaws. Dog food, hamster food, fish food, it was all just grub to Hannibal the bulldog. Eddie looked at Hannibal and wondered.

"Hannibal, you didn't eat little Mango, did you?" he asked.

Hannibal swished his old tail across the

floor and panted encouragingly at Eddie. That didn't necessarily mean anything. Besides, Hannibal on his wooden chariot sounded like a thunderstorm when he trundled around the hospital, so Mango would probably have heard and run away. Hopefully. Where would a hamster go? Where could he hide?

Eddie went to the rest room. Ron was having his afternoon cuppa and a biscuit. Eddie noticed Ron now had a new biscuit container – a tin one with a tight lid. No more dodgy currants for him.

"Ron, if you were a hamster where would you hide?"

Ron thought for a moment.

"I'd get a false passport and go to Brazil," he said, and chuckled to himself.

It wasn't often that Ron made a joke. Eddie smiled just to please Ron, and because he wanted a proper answer.

"Serious," said Eddie.

Ron thought again.

"Laundry," he said.

"Checked," said Eddie.

"Storeroom."

"Checked."

"Cupboards, drawers."

"Checked."

"Then you got one very lost hamster," said Ron.

Eddie tried Chelsea in Reception. Her bad mood had melted a bit. She was often annoyed with Eddie, but it never lasted that long.

"You've done your best, Eds," she said, "and we've all kept a careful lookout, but he's just . . . vanished."

Just then the front doors opened and in walked Kate with another little girl. Eddie would have expected her to be upset, but the girl was smiling and held a

small animal carrier. Eddie went to meet them.

"This is Aruna," said Kate.

"Hi," said Eddie.

"Hi! Where's Mango? I can't wait to see him again," said Aruna.

"Eddie will go and get him. Won't you, Eds? said Kate, smiling sweetly at Eddie.

Chapter Thirteen
EDDIE THINKS FAST

Eddie stared at Kate, not quite believing what he'd just heard. Kate's smile didn't waver.

"What you waiting for, Eds. Go on. Get Mango," she said.

Not for the first, nor for the last time in his life, Kate had well and truly dropped him in it. Either she really

believed that Eddie would have found Mango by now, or she wanted to have nothing to do with the possibility of failure, and disappointing Aruna. Probably a bit of all those things, but that didn't change the fact that Eddie was up to his neck in it.

He smiled at Aruna, then looked back at Kate. He could feel Chelsea behind the desk, listening and watching. A man with a chihuahua on his lap watched them, the little dog's eyes as wide as saucepan lids.

"Right," said Eddie. "I'll just, just go and . . ."

"Can I come too? I'd love to see round the hospital," said Aruna.

"No, no! You can't do that. There's, there's a . . . vicious animal just come in and strangers mustn't be allowed in case it . . . bites them. It's already attacked

Ron, the driver, hasn't it, Chelsea?"

"What? Oh, yes. Poor old Ron. He might never walk again," said Chelsea, trying to back up Eddie.

At that moment Ron walked through Reception, whistling.

"Night all," he said.

"Night," said Chelsea.

"Night," said Eddie.

"Night, Ron," said Kate.

Why did she do it? Sometimes Kate was a complete mystery to Eddie.

"That was Ron?" asked Aruna, getting confused. "But I thought you said . . ."

"Oh no. That's . . . the other Ron, isn't it?" said Eddie.

"Yes. The second Ron," said Chelsea.

"How many Rons are there?" asked Aruna.

"Oh. Just the two," said Eddie.

"Oh. I see, I think. But if there's a vicious animal in there, are the other animals safe? Is Mango alright?" asked Aruna.

"Oh yes, perfectly safe. It's just people this . . . vicious animal doesn't like," said Eddie.

Eddie had now committed himself to the lie. Somehow it had just happened. He had the opportunity to just tell Aruna straight: "Sorry, but Mango is missing," but he hadn't taken it. So often with Kate, before you knew it you were a part of something you didn't start and had no idea how to finish. Luckily, Chelsea stepped in to help. She too had somehow been caught in Kate's snare.

"Eddie, why don't you and Kate go and . . . er, get Mango, and I'll show Aruna how we run the hospital. It's pretty

quiet at the moment, so I can spare the time," said Chelsea.

"Right. Thanks," said Eddie, grabbing Kate by the shoulder.

"Be careful that vicious animal doesn't get you," said Aruna.

"We'll be very careful," said Eddie.

"What is it?" asked Aruna.

"What's what?"

"The vicious animal."

"Ah. Actually, it's a girl-eating crocodile. I might let it have Kate for it's tea," said Eddie, dragging Kate through into the corridor.

"Why didn't you tell her?" hissed Eddie, when they were in the corridor.

"Tell her what?" asked Kate.

"That I haven't found Mango, of course."

"You've had loads of time to find him.

Anyway, you could have told Aruna when we arrived that Mango was still lost. Why didn't *you*?" said Kate.

"Because . . . just because," said Eddie.

"And that's why I didn't. Just because," said Kate, as if she had just proved her point.

There was no time to argue. They had to have one last big effort to find Mango, otherwise there was going to be one very unhappy little girl in Reception.

Chapter Fourteen

UNEXPECTED HELP

Eddie found Greg and Kalim and explained the situation. They both agreed to help. There were four of them now and they agreed to split and search different areas of the hospital. Kalim and Greg would search the wards. Eddie would take the storeroom and the operating theatre and Kate would

take the laundry room and the rest room. Hilary David was out on calls and Mr Wensleydale was still trying to do his paperwork. They were all in agreement that the less he knew about this the better. They started their search.

Eddie looked again in each cupboard in the storeroom. He opened boxes of bedding and checked each one for Mango-sized bite holes. He looked under the sink, behind the pipes. He went to the operating theatre and looked on every clean and polished surface, under every surface, hunted for cracks in windows and walls, for even the slightest clue that Mango had been this way. It was useless.

The four of them met back in the ward fifteen minutes later, and none of them had seen Mango. The kitten

looked through the mesh of its cage at them. Two dogs, both in for leg injuries, looked from their cages. The much-recovered squirrel chewed a nut thoughtfully as he watched them. Emma sat in her bed looking adoringly at Eddie. Hannibal squatted and slobbered in his sleep, blissfully unaware that there had even been a search. In a corner was the cage from which Mango had escaped.

"I'll go and tell Aruna," said Eddie.

"Kalim or I should do that," said Greg. "It's our job. Go on, you've done enough."

"OK. Thanks," said Eddie.

Greg left the room. Eddie went and sat with Emma. He stroked her head and gave her a kiss on her snout.

"Poor little Mango, poor Hammy," said Eddie.

Emma got up and went over to Mango's cage and sniffed. Then she looked over at Eddie. It was enough.

"Stop Greg! Just stop him from saying anything to Aruna!" said Eddie.

Kate responded quickly and ran down the corridor. Eddie went to Emma and pointed at Mango's cage.

"Emma! Find Hammy! Where's Hammy? Where's Mango? Good girl, find Hammy! Go on!"

In Reception, Greg found Chelsea showing Aruna some of the patients' records on the computer. He introduced himself.

"Hi. Aruna?"

She nodded.

"I'm Greg. Listen. About Mango. I have something to tell you."

Kate rushed through the doors.

"Yes! It's about Mango. He's just being . . . given a last check over by one of the vets. Just to make sure he's alright."

Aruna looked at Kate and wondered just what was going on here.

Emma sniffed Mango's cage and bedding to get the scent, then sniffed all round the ward. Eddie encouraged her all the way.

"Good girl! Find Hammy! Where's Hammy?"

Emma went through to the operating theatre, looked inside and came out again. She went to the storeroom and sniffed through everything.

"Eddie, I don't think this is going to lead anywhere," Kalim said.

Eddie ignored her.

"Come on, Em. Good girl. Where's

Hammy?"

Emma finished sniffing around the storeroom and set off down the corridor, Eddie and Kalim following. She seemed to be heading for the rest room, then stopped suddenly outside Mr Wensleydale's room. It was slightly open and Emma nosed it open further and entered.

"Uh oh! Trouble," said Eddie, as he followed. Kalim followed him.

Mr Wensleydale looked up from his paperwork.

"What's this? A convention being held in my room that I didn't know about. Kalim, what is . . . what is Emma up to?"

Emma was sniffing Mr Wensleydale: his shoes and his legs and his shirt.

"Have I robbed a bank or something? What is going on?" he said.

"You're not . . . I mean, you're not concealing a hamster about your person, are you, Mr Wensleydale?" asked Eddie.

Kalim wanted to laugh, but Mr Wensleydale's stern look made it clear that anything resembling a smile would be a bad idea.

Emma suddenly switched her attention to the desk and sniffed the drawer where Mango had made his nest. Then she sniffed across the floor and towards Mr Wensleydale's white surgeon's coat which hung on the door. Emma sniffed the coat enthusiastically and tried to get her nose in the pocket. She turned to Eddie and whined.

"What is that dog doing?" asked Mr Wensleydale,

Eddie went to the coat and looked in the pocket. A pair of small, dark,

glittering eyes peered back, then Mango gave a huge yawn which almost split his jaw. He had woken up and now he was hungry. Eddie hugged Emma. She was a heroine.

Ten minutes later, the look on Aruna's face made it clear that all the trouble had been worthwhile. She stroked Mango happily.

"Do you know? For a minute I thought you'd lost him and didn't know how to tell me. Isn't that dopey?" she said.

Eddie laughed.

"As if we'd do that," he said.

"He does go missing – a lot. He's like that. He especially likes to snuggle in people's pockets. That's always the first place to look," said Aruna.

On his way home, Eddie thought about just how much could happen in such a short time. Maybe his wishing he could hibernate, like Charlie, wasn't such a great idea after all. In six months, all sorts of things could happen: new animals to meet; lots of trouble to get Kate into; new ways to tease Greg and occasionally put one over on Old Cheesy. Maybe Emma would be playing for England in six months – England's dog team that is! No, life was for living, not for sleeping . . . for humans, anyway.

Enjoy a sneak preview from

Rainbow
ANIMAL HOSPITAL

Flame Fights Back

Available now!

The car bumped along the muddy track, brambles scratching its side. Hilary David, one of the vets from the Rainbow Animal Hospital, sat hunched over the steering wheel, her knuckles white from gripping it so tightly. Beside her was Eddie Wright, watching the track ahead with as much concentration as Hilary. The car, a battered Fiat Panda, gave a violent lurch as it hit a rock and Eddie fell against the door. He tightened his seat belt. He hoped they would be in time.

He could tell from the tight lines on Hilary's face that she had her doubts. And if they were too late, what would they find? What would have happened? Farmer Draper had said that she might make it. She might not.

They turned a bend and there, about a quarter of a mile ahead, was Meadow

Farm. Hilary put her foot down and the car lurched faster.

"Proper little Damon Hill, aren't you?" said Eddie. "You only have two speeds – fast and very fast."

Eddie knew he could cheek Hilary because she wasn't even listening. She turned briefly to him and said: "I know you want to watch, but I may need you to help too. If I ask you to do something, just do it. No questions. Right?"

"Right," said Eddie.

Hilary meant business.

The farm was a shambles. All the fencing and gates were broken, and rusting machinery was lying around. Farmer Draper had the reputation for being a bit of a skinflint and judging, by the look of the farm, he hadn't spent

much on its upkeep for some time. As the car screeched to a halt, he came out of a barn. He was a large man with pork-chop whiskers and a battered trilby hat that looked as if he never took it off, even when he went to bed. He was wearing a dirty old apron which was smeared with blood. He was wiping his hands on a cloth.

"So much for hygiene," Hilary hissed between her teeth. "Come on, Eddie. Action stations!"

The three of them trudged through the mud to the barn. From inside came a whinny and a puffing sound that meant someone was in great pain.

It was cold in the barn. A single light bulb hung from a wire, providing a small shaft of light. The rest was in shadow and the place smelled of ancient hay, muck and cows. Lying on her side

under the weak pool of light was a large chestnut horse, her belly swollen, in labour. Her coat was damp and sweating, and steam was rising from it. The eye Eddie saw was large and wild – the eye of panic. She tried to move but the effort was immense and the pain greater – her whinnying sounded like a scream. Two cows were looking over from an adjacent stall. Both chewed occasionally, but were too engrossed in watching Bess to do anything else. Eddie wanted to look away but he made himself face the great horse. She might need him.

Hilary approached slowly and let the horse get a good look at her face. She stroked her flanks soothingly, then her muzzle, cooing and whispering to her: "Good girl, there we go, good Bess."

She turned to Farmer Draper.

"How long has she been in labour?" she asked.

"Oh, I reckon . . . about five hours," he said, tilting his hat back on his head to reveal a great bald dome, pink and smooth as a baby's.

"Then why didn't you call me before? She's in a lot of pain!" said Hilary, barely concealing the anger she felt.

"Didn't know she was that bad. I can't be calling out the vet every five minutes, not at forty quid a throw."

Hilary decided it was best to say nothing more. Besides, she didn't have time to argue – she was going to be too busy. Bess had lost a lot of blood and was in a great deal of pain. Hilary opened her bag and took out a syringe. She measured out some painkiller – enough to help but not too much or Bess might become unconscious and

therefore unable to help with the birth of her foal. Hilary injected Bess, then turned to Eddie.

"What I want you to do is comfort her. I need to find out what's going wrong and the more relaxed Bess is the better. OK?"

"Right," said Eddie.

He knelt beside Bess's great head and looked at the foam and mucus on the hay, the wet mouth and the wild eye. He stroked her muzzle and made small 'shhhhhh' noises. The eye looked at him from a long way off, then rolled back again into Bess's pain.

"Is he qualified? Looks too young to me," said Farmer Draper.

"You don't need to be qualified to comfort an animal," said Hilary. "Of course, you could always do it if you prefer."

"He'll do. I suppose," said Farmer Draper.

Eddie continued to stroke Bess, aware of the large moony eyes of the cows behind him. The painkiller had taken hold a little, but only to ease, not eradicate the pain. Bess was taking small, exhausted breaths. She could not keep it up for much longer. The foal was caught sideways inside Bess, which meant that it could not be born properly.

"The foal is breached, Mr Draper. Stuck fast. I can feel it. I'm not sure that I can save it," said Hilary, looking up at the farmer.

Rainbow
ANIMAL HOSPITAL
Steve Attridge

Sick pets and injured animals –
every day brings a new emergency for Eddie
and the staff at the Rainbow Animal Hospital.

Bartholomew the Champion

When a huge Bernese Mountain Dog with a broken
leg fails to get better, only Eddie realises what's
wrong. He and his brilliant little sister Kate
come up with a daring plan to save the dog's life.
It could get them into serious trouble but that's
a risk they have to take – for Bartholomew's sake.

If you care about animals and
love adventure stories,

Rainbow
ANIMAL HOSPITAL

is for you.

Collins
HarperCollins*Publishers*

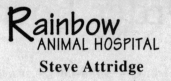

Rainbow
ANIMAL HOSPITAL

Steve Attridge

Sick pets and injured animals –
every day brings a new emergency for Eddie
and the staff at Rainbow Animal Hospital.

Trash Cat's Secret

Eddie is surprised to see his best friend's cat
being brought into the hospital. What has she
been eating? The hospital floods during a storm,
there's a power cut, and a routine operation turns
into a fight for life. But it is not only Trash
who's in danger. Eddie and Kate have to move fast if
all the other animals are going to be rescued, too.

If you care about animals and
love adventure stories,

Rainbow
ANIMAL HOSPITAL

is for you.

Collins
HarperCollins*Publishers*

Order Form

To order direct from the publishers, just make a list of the titles you want and fill in the form below:

Name

....

Address

....

....

....

Send to: Dept 6, HarperCollins Publishers Ltd, Westerhill Road, Bishopbriggs, Glasgow G64 2QT.

Please enclose a cheque or postal order to the value of the cover price, plus:

UK & BFPO: Add £1.00 for the first book, and 25p per copy for each additional book ordered.

Overseas and Eire: Add £2.95 service charge. Books will be sent by surface mail but quotes for airmail despatch will be given on request.

A 24-hour telephone ordering service is available to Visa and Access card holders: 0141- 772 2281